SECRETS OF THE LIBRARY OF DOOM

INVISIBLE INK

BY MICHAEL DAHL
ILLUSTRATED BY PATRICIO CLAREY

STONE ARCH BOOKS
a capstone imprint

Secrets of the Library of Doom is published by
Stone Arch Books, an imprint of Capstone.
1710 Roe Crest Drive
North Mankato, Minnesota 56003
www.capstonepub.com

Library of Congress Cataloging-in-Publication Data is
available on the Library of Congress website.

ISBN: 978-1-4965-9720-5 (hardcover)
ISBN: 978-1-4965-9899-8 (paperback)
ISBN: 978-1-4965-9739-7 (ebook PDF)

Summary: The Eraser, sworn enemy of the Library of Doom,
has created a powerful gas that turns ink invisible, making
all books empty and useless. Will the Librarian be able to
stop the villain's wicked scheme?

Designed by Hilary Wacholz

Printed and bound in the USA.
PA117

TABLE OF CONTENTS

The Library of Doom is a hidden fortress.
It holds the world's largest collection
of strange and dangerous books.

Behold the Librarian. He defends the Library—and
the world—from super-villains, clever thieves,
and fierce monsters. Many of his adventures
have remained secret. Now they can be told.

SECRET #99
YOU DON'T ALWAYS HAVE TO SEE
SOMETHING TO KNOW IT'S THERE.

Chapter One

INVISIBLE INC.

Night covers the city. Wind **BLOWS** through the dark alleys.

The FULL moon above the city is as blank as an empty page.

In one alley, the wind STIRS up dead leaves. They skitter in front of a small building.

The windows are **DARK**.

A sign hangs above the door. It reads:

INVISIBLE INC.

The sign **SWINGS** back and forth, creaking.

REAKKK REAKKK REEAAAKKKK!

The door to the building suddenly opens.

A strange man steps out.

His hair is wild. His eyes are hidden by **THICK** glasses.

REAKKK REAKKK REEAAAKKKK!

The man glances up at the noisy sign.

Then he pulls something from his coat. It is a weird SPRAY bottle.

The man aims the bottle at the sign.
He sprays a thick green **GAS**.

The GAS wraps around the sign.

The words on the sign begin to fade. Soon, they are gone.

"Invisible Inc. is now invisible ink," whispers the man.

He hides the bottle back in his coat. Then he hurries down the ALLEY.

Chapter Two

THE HEAD IN THE WINDOW

Not far away, a young man **LOOKS** through a store window.

"That's it!" he says to himself. "There is *The Floating Head*!"

The young man **RUSHES** into the
bookstore.

Piles of OLD books cover the floor.
More books fill the shelves.

The young man turns to the main
window. He reaches out to grab *The
Floating Head*.

"AAAHHHHH!" he screams.

A head with WILD hair is floating in the darkness outside. It is staring at him.

The door to the bookstore opens.

A strange man with WILD hair walks
inside.

The stranger looks at the young man.
He gives a wide SMILE.

"I hope I did not **SCARE** you," the
stranger says.

The young man **SHRUGS**. "It was nothing," he says.

The young man hands his book to the store clerk. He pulls out several bills and hands them to her too.

"You are right," says the stranger. "It *is* nothing!"

Chapter Three

GONE OR INVISIBLE?

The stranger pulls out a weird bottle. He aims it into the store and **SPRAYS**.

FFFSSSSSSSSHHHHHHH!

A thick green **GAS** covers the books and the people.

When the GAS clears, the stranger
is gone.

"What was that all about?" asks the
young man. He COUGHS as he grabs
his book.

"Wait a minute," says the clerk. "The ink has disappeared from your money! These bills are just blank paper!"

The young man **FLIPS** through his book. "All the pages are empty!" he says.

Chapter Four

PURPLE GAS

A woman **SCREAMS** outside the bookstore.

The young man rushes into the **ALLEY**.

"My bike!" the woman shouts. "Someone **STOLE** the license plates!"

The strange man with the SPRAY bottle stands nearby. He smiles.

"They are still there," the man says. "Only now the numbers and letters are invisible!"

The young man looks at the street sign on the corner. "The sign is blank too," he whispers.

The woman stares at something else. "Is that a man in the sky?" she asks.

The stranger quickly looks up. "No!" he **SCREAMS** into the sky. "You can't stop me, Librarian!"

The flying LIBRARIAN lands in the alley. The light from a streetlamp shines off his dark glasses.

The Librarian points at the stranger. "Give up, Eraser," he says. "Your plan to **DESTROY** all of earth's books won't work."

The WILD-haired Eraser shouts, "That's what you think! When I find your Library, your books will be truly doomed!"

The Eraser pushes a hidden button on his bottle. A huge cloud of purple GAS sprays out.

The **GAS** wraps around the Librarian.

"Now *you're* invisible," the Eraser laughs.

Chapter Five

BLINDED BY THE LIGHT

The purple **GAS** clears. The Librarian is gone. Only his glasses can be seen hanging in the air.

The Librarian's voice **ECHOES** through the alley. "Here's some *light* reading!" he says.

The light shining off the Librarian's glasses grows brighter. And brighter.

Light **BURSTS** out from the glasses like rays of sunlight.

ZZZZZZZZZSSSSSSSS!!!!

The light **BURNS** into the motorcycle's license plates. It blasts the street sign.

Light blazes into the bookstore's windows.

"My books!" the clerk **SHOUTS** from inside the store. "All the words are <u>back</u> in my books!"

The blinding light fades away.

The alley is **DARK** again. But the license plates and the street sign are back to normal.

The light brought back all the **MISSING** letters and words.

The LIBRARIAN is back too. He holds the Eraser's shoulder.

"I can't move!" yells the Eraser. "It feels like a **CHAIN** is wrapped around me!"

"Yes, it is an invisible chain," says the Librarian. "Or, you might call them *invisible links*."

FWWWWOOOOSHHH!

The Librarian **FLIES** back into the air
with the Eraser.

The young man looks down at the cover
of *The Floating Head*.

Then he looks up at the hero. "Now *that*
guy should be in a book!" he says.

GLOSSARY

alley (AL-ee)—a small path between buildings

blaze (BLAYZ)—to shine brightly

clerk (KLURK)—someone who works at a store

disappear (dis-uh-PEER)—to pass out of sight

glance (GLANSS)—to look quickly at something

inc. (INK)—short for the word *incorporated*; it is part of the name of many companies

invisible (in-VIZ-uh-buhl)—not possible to see

license plate (LEYE-suhns PLAYT)—a metal plate on a car or motorcycle that has a series of numbers and letters that is used to identify the vehicle and who it belongs to

links (LINX)—the small metal loops that make up a chain

weird (WEERD)—very strange and not normal

TALK ABOUT IT

1. The story takes place at night. What feeling does that create? How would the story be different if it took place during the day?

2. How would you describe the Eraser? How does he act? What is his goal? Use examples from the text to back up your answer.

WRITE ABOUT IT

1. Imagine if all the ink in your school and home became invisible. Write a paragraph about how life would be different. If you'd like, write a story about how you return everything to normal.

2. The Eraser has a green gas that makes ink invisible and a purple gas that makes people disappear. What other kinds of gas might be in the bottle? Write about what they do.

ABOUT THE AUTHOR

Michael Dahl is an award-winning author of more than 200 books for young people. He especially likes to write scary or weird fiction. His latest series are the sci-fi adventure Escape from Planet Alcatraz and School Bus of Horrors. As a child, he spent lots of time in libraries. "The creepier, the better," he says. These days, besides writing, he likes traveling and hunting for the one, true door that leads to the Library of Doom.

ABOUT THE ILLUSTRATOR

Patricio Clarey was born in 1978 in Argentina. He graduated in fine arts from the Martín A. Malharro School of Visual Arts, specializing in illustration and graphic design. Patricio currently lives in Barcelona, Spain, where he works as a freelance graphic designer and illustrator. He has created several comics and graphic novels, and his work has been featured in books and other publications.